The Planets and Pluto

By Julie Haydon

T0342755

Contents

The Planets

There are eight planets in the Solar System. Each planet is large enough that its own gravity pulls it into a round shape. Each planet orbits the Sun in a path it has cleared of other space objects.

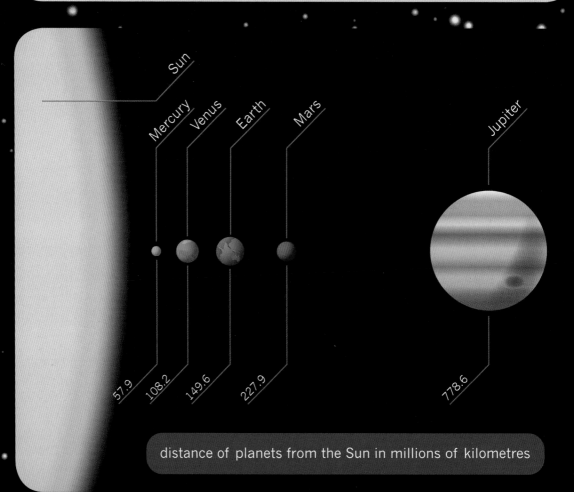

Sun

Mercury Venus Earth Mars Jupiter

57.9 108.2 149.6 227.9 778.6

distance of planets from the Sun in millions of kilometres

The Sun is a star and it gives the planets light and heat energy. The planets and the Sun are part of the Milky Way Galaxy.

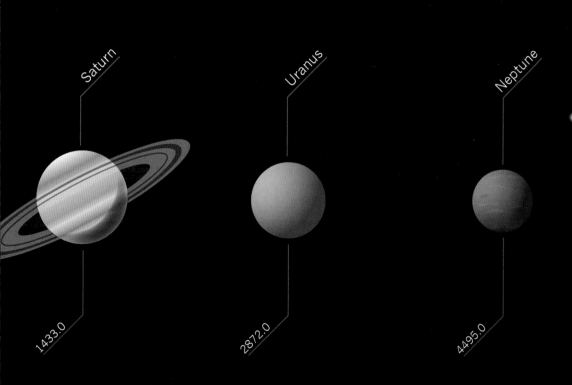

Saturn

1433.0

Uranus

2872.0

Neptune

4495.0

The four inner planets, Mercury, Venus, Earth and Mars, are closest to the Sun. These planets are small and are made up mostly of rock.

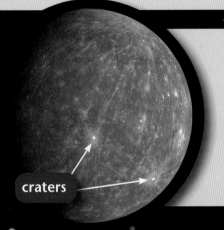

craters

Mercury is the smallest planet in the Solar System. It orbits the Sun more quickly than the other planets. It is extremely hot during the day, almost airless and is covered in huge craters.

Venus is the brightest natural object in the sky, after the Sun and the Moon. It is similar in size to Earth.

Earth is the only planet known to contain life. Water covers 71 per cent of Earth's surface.

Mars is known as the 'red planet' because its surface is covered in rust-coloured dust.

The four outer planets, Jupiter, Saturn, Uranus and Neptune, are giant planets made up mainly of gases. They are known as the 'gas giants'.

Jupiter is the largest planet in the Solar System. It is made up of gas and liquid but scientists believe that it may have a solid core.

Saturn is surrounded by many rings that are made up of ice and rock. Saturn also has more than 50 moons.

rings

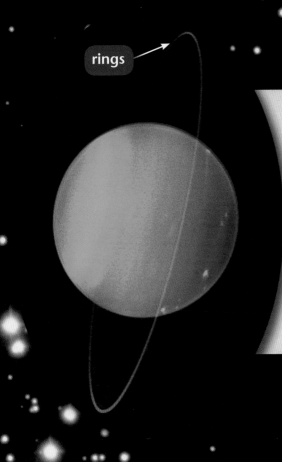

rings

Uranus has many rings and moons, too. Uranus looks blue-green in colour and it rotates on its side. Many scientists think that a collision with an Earth-sized space object may have knocked Uranus on its side soon after it was formed.

Neptune is the planet furthest from the Sun and has the fastest winds in the Solar System. Neptune cannot be seen from Earth without a telescope.

Pluto

Pluto was once thought to be the ninth planet in the Solar System. However, because it does not orbit in a clear path around the Sun, Pluto is now called a dwarf planet.

the Milky Way

There are eight planets in the Solar System – Mercury, Venus, Earth, Mars, Jupiter, Saturn, Uranus and Neptune. The Sun and these eight planets are part of the Milky Way Galaxy.

ASTRONOMY NEWS

July 2020

Pluto – A Dwarf Planet

Pluto is a dwarf planet in the Solar System. It was discovered in 1930 by a young astronomer who was working at an observatory in the USA. The planet was named after the Roman god of the underworld.

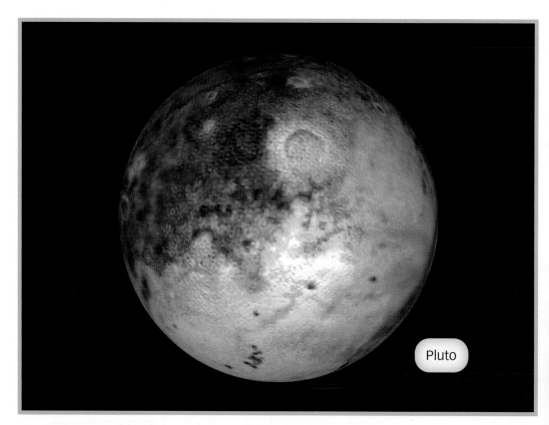

Pluto

a powerful telescope at an observatory

Pluto is dark and cold because its average distance from the Sun is about 5.9 billion kilometres. One day on Pluto is about as long as six days on Earth. This dwarf planet takes about 248 Earth years to orbit the Sun. Pluto is so far away from Earth that a person needs a powerful telescope to see it in the night sky.

With a diameter of about 2400 kilometres, Pluto is smaller than Earth's Moon. The Moon's diameter is 3475 kilometres and Earth's diameter is 12756 kilometres.

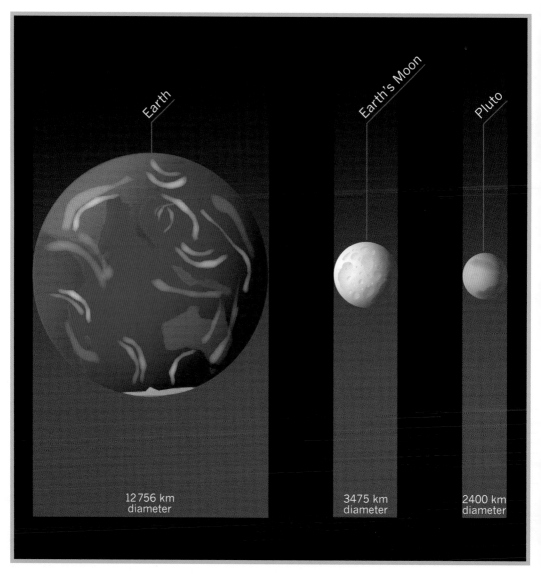

Earth

Earth's Moon

Pluto

12756 km
diameter

3475 km
diameter

2400 km
diameter

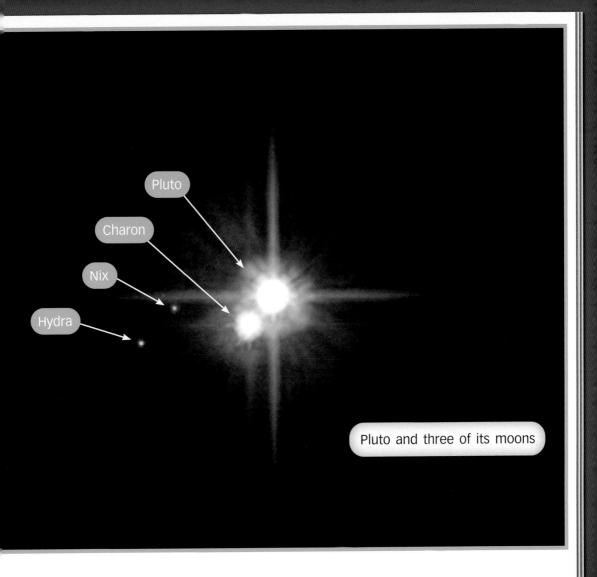

Pluto

Charon

Nix

Hydra

Pluto and three of its moons

Charon, the largest of Pluto's five moons, was discovered in 1978. Pluto's four other moons are Nix, Hydra, Kerberos and Styx.

Unlike Jupiter, Saturn, Uranus and Neptune, Pluto does not have planetary rings.

Pluto is part of an enormous ring of cold and rocky objects in space beyond Neptune, called the Kuiper Belt. The Kuiper Belt orbits the Sun.

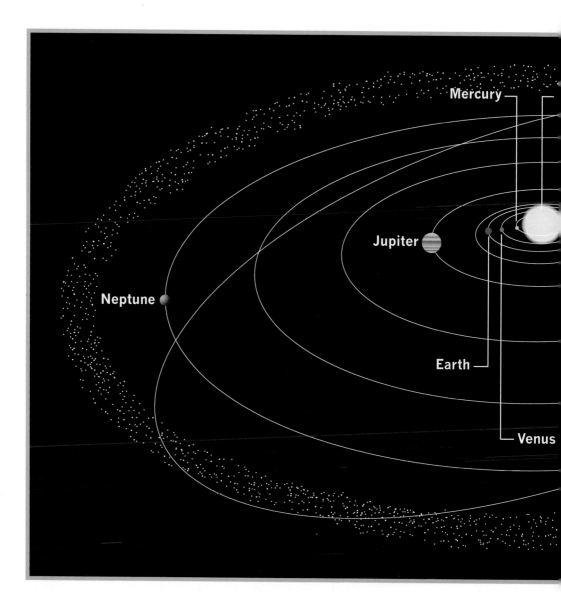

Before being given the title of dwarf planet in August 2006, Pluto was known as the ninth and smallest planet of the Solar System.

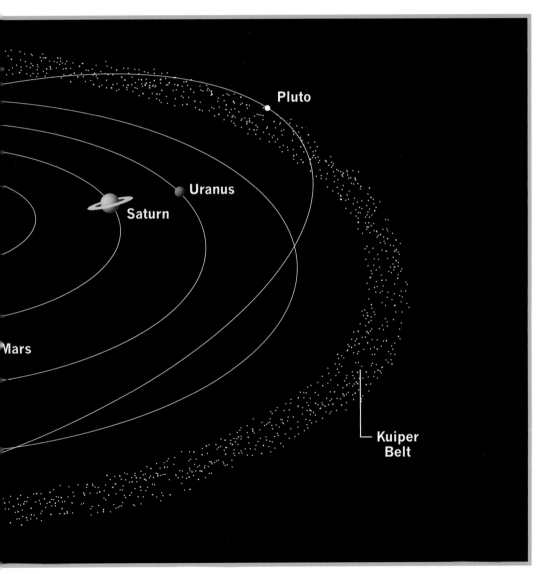

Recently, scientists decided that because Pluto is part of the Kuiper Belt and has not created a clear path as it orbits the Sun, it should not be called a planet.

Pluto and its largest moon, Charon, seen through the Hubble Telescope